My "a" Sound Box®

(This book concentrates on the short "a" sound in the story line. Words beginning with the long "a" sound are included at the end of the book.)

Library of Congress Cataloging-in-Publication Data
Moncure, Jane Belk.
My "a" sound box / by Jane Belk Moncure; illustrated by Colin King.
p. cm.
Summary: A little boy fills his sound box with words beginning with the letter "a."
ISBN 1-56766-767-8 (lib. reinforced : alk. paper)
[1. Alphabet.] I. King, Colin, ill. II. Title.
PZ7.M739 My   2000
[E]—dc21   99-056558

My "a" Sound Box

Jane Belk Moncure

illustrated by Colin King

The Child's World

Little  had a box.

"I will find things that begin with my 'a' sound," he said.

"I will put them into
my sound  box."

Little 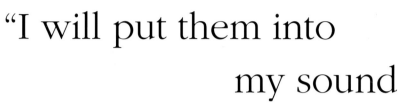 put on his hat and went
for a walk.

He found apples,
apples,
apples.

Did he put the apples into his box?

He did.

Little  found an alligator.

Did he put the alligator into the box with the apples? He did.

Little found ants,

ants,

ants.

Did he put the ants into the box with the apples and the alligator?

He did.

Then Little  found arrows,

arrows,

arrows.

Guess where he put the arrows?

Next, Little  found an ax.

It was a toy ax.

Guess where he put the ax?

Now the box was so full . . .

the ants, 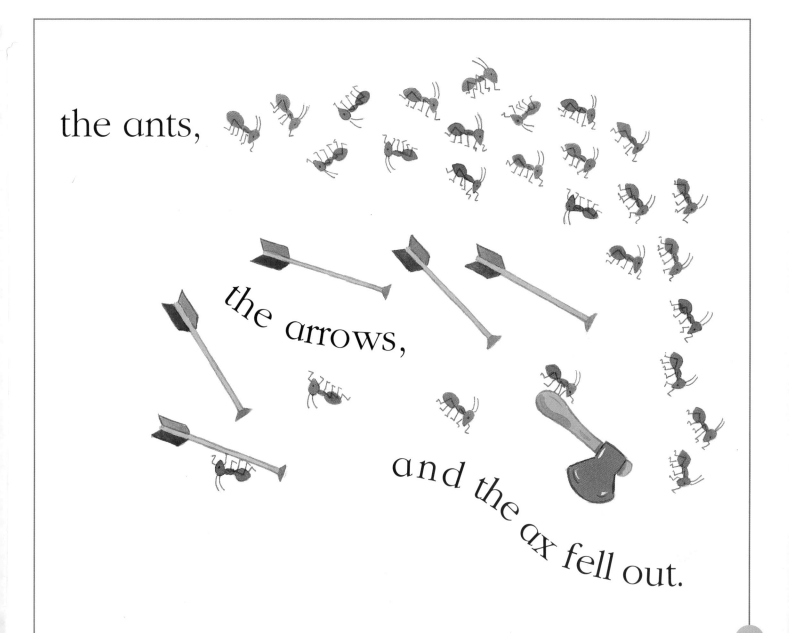 the arrows, and the ax fell out.

The apples

and the alligator

fell out, too.

"Now who will help me
fill my box?" said Little a.

Just then, an astronaut came by.

"I will help you,"

said the astronaut.

"We will fill your box."

Guess what happened next?

The astronaut took

Little  for a ride.

Up, up, and away!

ants

alligator

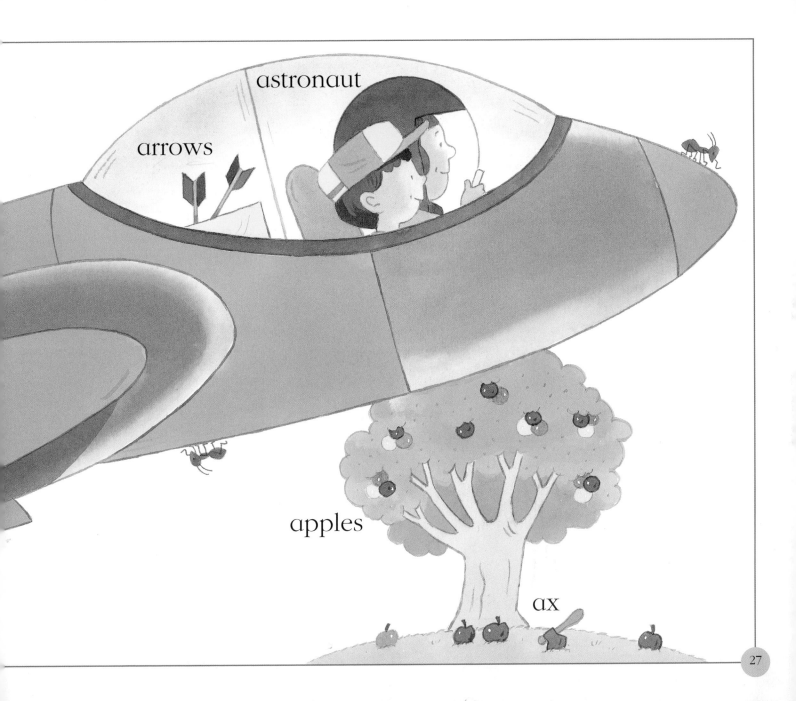

arrows

astronaut

apples

ax

Can you read these words
with Little  ?

antelope

acrobat

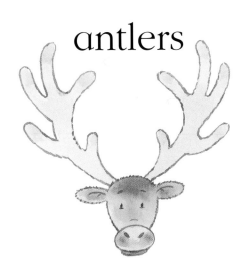

antlers

anchor

animals

ambulance

Little  has another sound in some words.

He says his name, "a."

Can you read these words?

Listen for Little 's name.

acorn

angel

ape

apron

April

ABOUT THE AUTHOR AND ILLUSTRATOR

Jane Belk Moncure began her writing career when she was in kindergarten. She has never stopped writing. Many of her children's stories and poems have been published, to the delight of young readers, including her son Jim, whose childhood experiences found their way into many of her books.

Mrs. Moncure's writing is based upon an active career in early childhood education. A recipient of an M.A. degree from Columbia University, Mrs. Moncure has taught and directed nursery, kindergarten, and primary grade programs in California, New York, Virginia, and North Carolina. As a former member of the faculties of Virginia Commonwealth University and the University of Richmond, she taught prospective teachers in early childhood education.

Mrs. Moncure has travelled extensively abroad, studying early childhood programs in the United Kingdom, The Netherlands, and Switzerland. She was the first president of the Virginia Association for Early Childhood Education and received its award for outstanding service to young children.

A resident of North Carolina, Mrs. Moncure is currently a full-time writer and educational consultant. She is married to Dr. James A. Moncure, former vice president of Elon College.

Colin King studied at the Royal College of Art, London. He started his freelance career as an illustrator, working for magazines and advertising agencies.

He began drawing pictures for children's books in 1976 and has illustrated over sixty titles to date.

Included in a wide variety of subjects are a best-selling children's encyclopedia and books about spies and detectives.

His books have been translated into several languages, including Japanese and Hebrew. He has four grown-up children and lives in Suffolk, England, with his wife, three dogs, and a cat.